# BEAUTIFUL MOON

## MOON

### A CHILD'S PRAYER

BY
TONYA BOLDEN

ILLUSTRATED BY
ERIC VELASQUEZ

ABRAMS BOOKS FOR YOUNG READERS · NEW YORK

The amber orb floats,
washing the night
with a radiant glow.

Stars hide.

Only city lights glitter.

It's not a silent night.

Car horns beep and blare.
There is music in the air.

And someone calls out,
"I love you!"

A little boy wakes up,
scrambles out of bed,
drops to his knees.

He forgot to say his prayers.

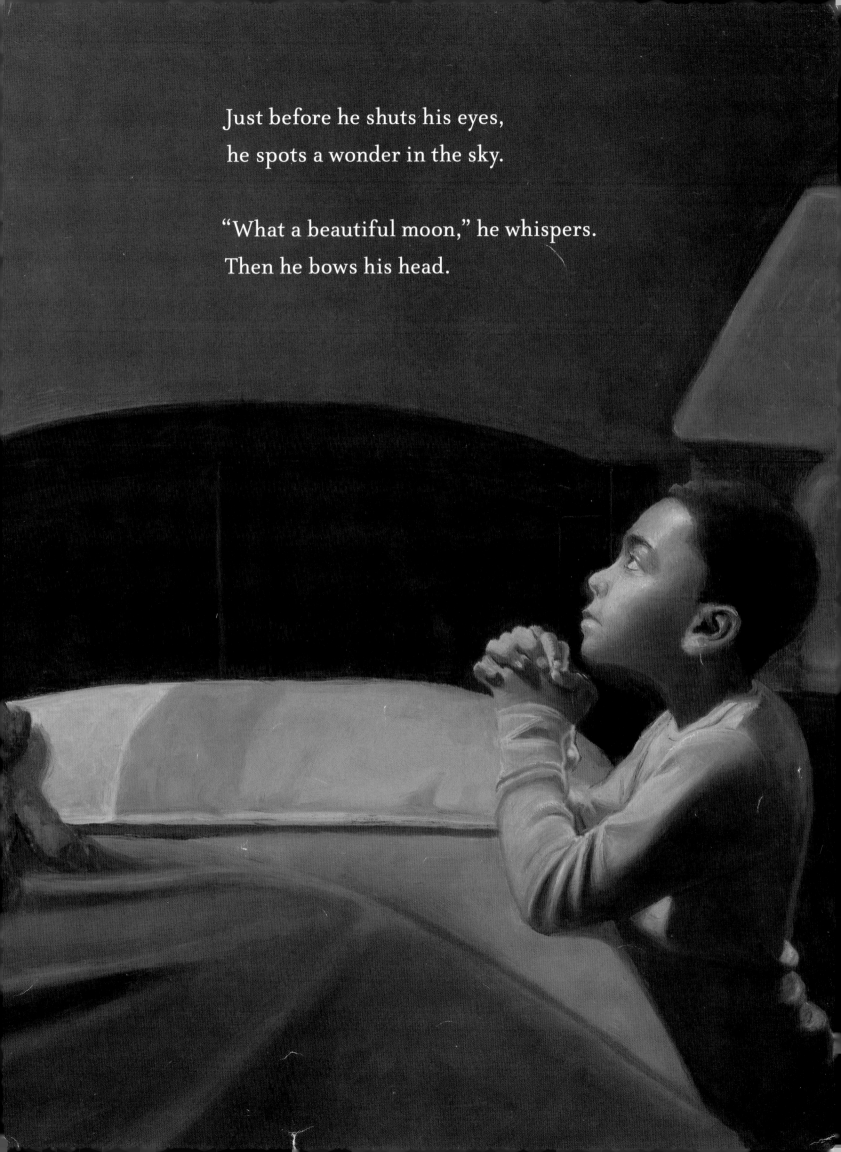

Just before he shuts his eyes,
he spots a wonder in the sky.

"What a beautiful moon," he whispers.
Then he bows his head.

Blocks away, a woman, bundled up,
a park bench her bed,
gazes at the beautiful moon,
willing herself warm.

The little boy prays for people with no homes.

Closer by, a man on a train
gives no heed to
night sights speeding by.

He does not see
the beautiful moon.

His mind is on his daughter,
a soldier in a distant land.

The little boy prays
for wars to end.

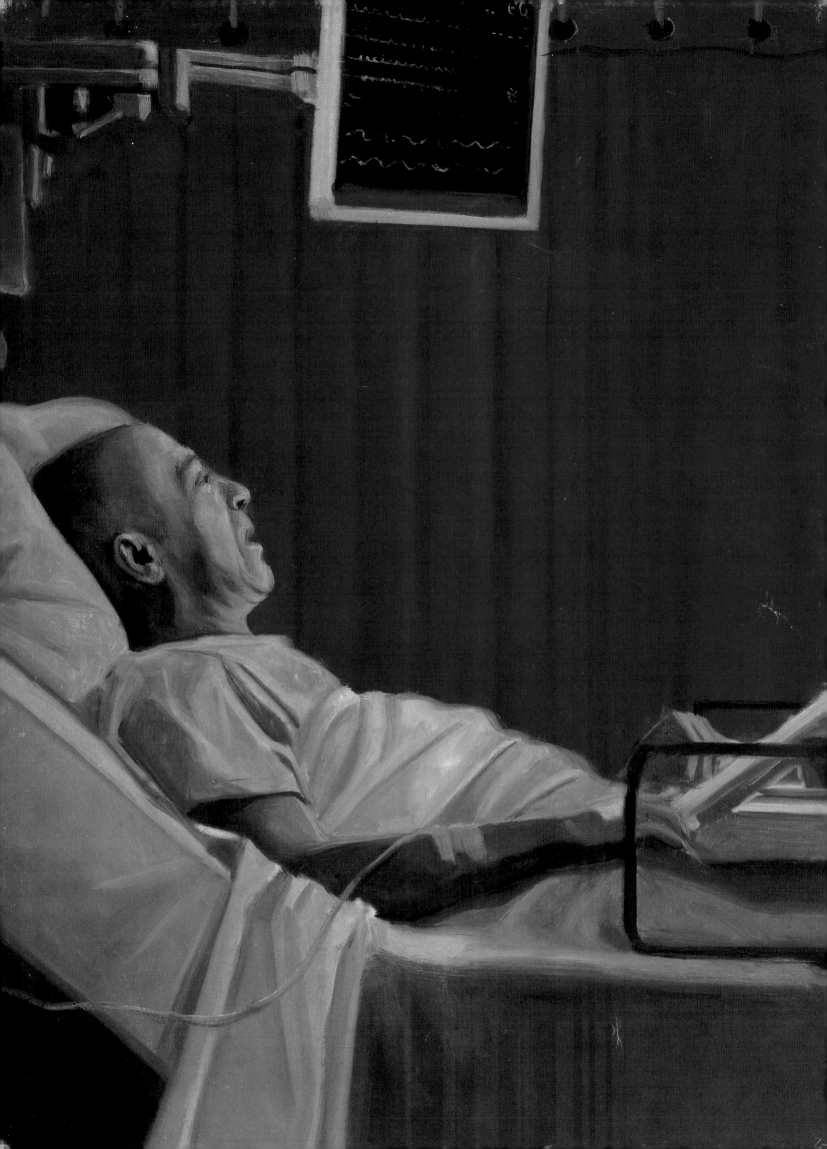

Across town, an old man
in a hospital room
wishes for a window,
imagining that if he could see
a starry night
or behold a beautiful moon,
he would slip into soothing sleep.

The little boy prays
for the sick to be healed.

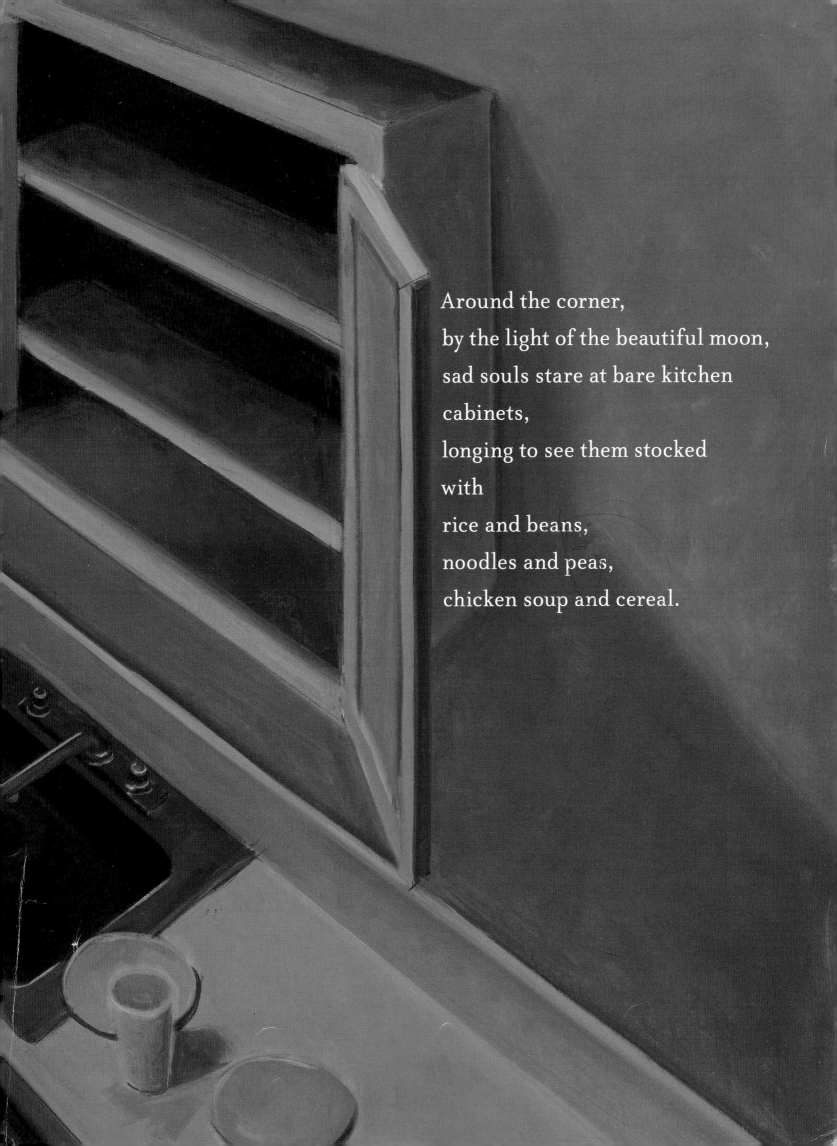

Around the corner,
by the light of the beautiful moon,
sad souls stare at bare kitchen
cabinets,
longing to see them stocked
with
rice and beans,
noodles and peas,
chicken soup and cereal.

The little boy prays
for people, little and big,
to have the food they need.

And the little boy prays
for Grandma Grace;

for Mommy, Daddy;
for his baby sister, Sydney;

for Mikey, his turtle;

for his teacher to read a story every day.

He promises that when tomorrow night comes,
he won't forget to pray.

And the beautiful moon goes on its way.

∞

TO ALL THOSE IN NEED OF PRAYER.
—T. B.

FOR RYAN, MAY YOU ALWAYS STAY AMAZED.
—E. V.

*The illustrations in this book were made in mixed media and oil on watercolor paper.*

Library of Congress Cataloging-in-Publication Data

Bolden, Tonya.
Beautiful moon : a child's prayer / by Tonya Bolden ; illustrated by Eric Velasquez.
pages cm
Summary: "Under a radiant moon and surrounded by all the noises of the city at night, a little boy prays for those in need, for wars to end, for the sick to be healed, and for all the members of his family"— Provided by publisher.
ISBN 978-1-4197-0792-6
[1. Prayer—Fiction. 2. Bedtime—Fiction. 3. City and town life—Fiction. 4. Moon—Fiction.] I. Velasquez, Eric, illustrator.
II. Title.
PZ7.B635855Be 2014
[E]—dc23
2013031976

Text copyright © 2014 Tonya Bolden
Illustrations copyright © 2014 Eric Velasquez
Book design by Maria T. Middleton

Printed and bound in China
10 9 8 7 6 5 4 3 2 1

Abrams Books for Young Readers are available at special discounts when purchased in quantity for premiums and promotions as well as fundraising or educational use. Special editions can also be created to specification. For details, contact specialsales@abramsbooks.com or the address below.

ABRAMS
THE ART OF BOOKS SINCE 1949
115 West 18th Street
New York, NY 10011
www.abramsbooks.com